A PG-13 Literary Magazine for readers of Young Adult Fiction

Fall 2016
Volume 4 Issue 2

Editor-Nichole Hansen
Editor-Tevin Hansen
Cover Art-Cesar Valtierra

Stinkwaves Magazine
PO Box 21843
Lincoln, NE 68542
www.stinkwavesmagazine.com
submissions@stinkwavesmagazine.com

Because adults don't give out stinkwaves . . . only children do that.

-Roald Dahl, *The Witches*

Stinkwaves Magazine Fall 2016
Volume 4 Issue 2
Copyright ©2016 Handersen Publishing LLC

All rights reserved.

All ownership of the submitted material belongs to the original writer or artist.

No part of this publication may be reproduced, distributed or transmitted in any form or by any means, or stored in a database or retrieval system without prior written consent from the author(s) or Publisher.

This is a work of fiction. Names, characters, places, and incidents are the products of the authors' imagination or are used fictitiously. Any resemblance to actual events, locales, or persons living or dead is entirely coincidental.

ISBN-10: 1-941429-41-6
ISBN-13: 978-1-941429-41-9

Handersen Publishing, LLC
Lincoln, Nebraska

WHAT'S INSIDE

WHAT'S INSIDE

FEATURED ARTISTS

Emma Donnelly

Skulls (1), Tombstone (13), Shadow (46), Flashlight (50),

Cemetery Gates (55)

Tevin Hansen

The Phantom in My Wardrobe (32-35)

A L Hayes

Tree (back cover), All Hallows Eve (14-25)

Denny Marshall

Floppy and Friends (10), Thing from the Closet (11),

Headlock (26), Break the Wall (31), Triangle Guy (49)

Linda and Niem

Cat Tree (6)

Cesar Valtierra

Lion (Cover), Ninja (4), Kart (37), Spider Baby (45),

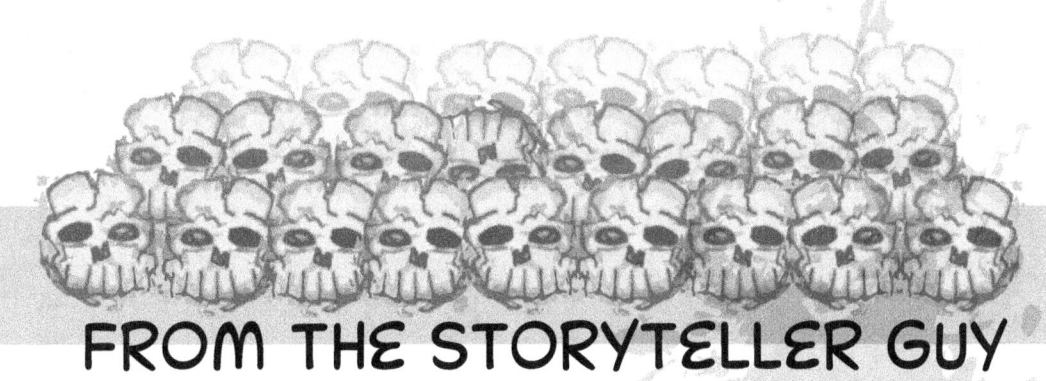

FROM THE STORYTELLER GUY

Are we ready for another Halloween? Another night of tricks and treats? Another round of Stinkwaves Magazine? Hard to believe that another year has gone by. But here we are in the midst of Halloween Twenty-Sixteen.

Seems like the spring issue of Stinkwaves has barely been out for a couple of months, and then KA-BOOM! Like the exhilarating but dangerous feeling of holding a Roman Candle in your hand, it is time to put together another issue—what is always our *favorite* issue to work on, the proudly corny titled: Halloween Spooktacular.

This year we omitted the subtitle in order to give your eyes a better chance to enjoy the awesome Lion cover, illustrated by Cesar Valtierra.

Imagine our surprise when we opened the submissions email and saw *that* crazy cool Lion staring back at us. We're always excited to read new short stories and poetry, but art submissions are about as rare as spotting Ogopogo (which is Canada's version of the elusive Loch Ness Monster). Give up the goods, Indie Artists! We know you've got some amazing stuff in your portfolios. Send it to us, or any other lit-mag out there. Just send it out there for the rest of us to enjoy! My wife and co-editor both looked at each other and said: "That's our cover."

Now, speaking of legends of the Great White North…

1

Growing up in Canada, Halloween was always taken very seriously—at least in our neighborhood. Unlike in America, where July 4th is the time for celebrating with fireworks, in Canada it is Halloween that's celebrated with nonstop firecrackers, jumping jacks, screecheroos, and all those wonderful (and annoying) explosions.

Other good times included Pumpkin Smashing. That's where you run up to a house (preferably not in your immediate neighborhood) and don't bother with candy, but instead bring joy to others by stomping your foot into the delicately carved face of a jack-o-lantern.

So many times I recall how me and my friends, all of us respectful, good-mannered, outstanding young citizens, would gratefully accept some free candy, with polite smiles on our painted faces or underneath our masks. We'd wait until the front door closed, count to five, then toss a stink bomb, or a smoke bomb, into the foyer of the house, then run off like happy little children.

Another cute example is how we would spot someone from school, an acquaintance perhaps, and discuss the evening while taking turns digging through their candy bag, complimenting them on all their great candy treasures. Then we'd walk away, waving and smiling, always with all their best treats in our hands, laughing and getting loaded up on more candy, candy, candy.

Hey, taking candy from kids smaller than you is *way* too easy, not to mention frowned upon even by the local hooligan population. Taking candy from someone your age, or even bigger than you, was always an honorable achievement. (Note: Never travel alone on Halloween because your candy will be in great danger of being pilfered.)

One of the most fun times, in between candy gorging and pumpkin smashing, was when someone would initiate a round of the traditional childhood game called "Human Bottle Rocket," where you held onto your bottle rocket, or several, and were deemed a *BWAAK-BWAAK! chicken* if you let it go before the BOOM at the end. Or Jumping Jack War, when you form a tight circle and light dozens of Jumping Jacks simultaneously, then kick them at each other. Extra fun if one actually took off while bouncing around.

Most times these silly childhood games were harmless, with a group of happy children lighting and throwing lit fireworks at each other (below the neckline, of course—for safety), or kicking the dancing firework around like some kind of pyromaniac version of hacky-sack. But every once in a while someone would hit their target.

Oh, how I merrily recall the time when one of our group ended up with a Jumping Jack dancing on his chest. I don't recall his name, but I certainly recall the funny dance moves, and all the colorful language he spewed forth as he boogied all around, desperately trying to remove his shirt that was apparently *just* loose enough for a lit Jumping Jack— which can last a good 10 seconds—to *zzzzzip!* straight up his costume.

After we stopped laughing hysterically and realized he was actually in a bit of pain, we helped him. His shirt came off, all right. Torn to shreds, by his friends, who were trying to "save his life."

Or the year my brother and I dressed up like ninjas. We even made our own ninja stars, using black tape and large nails. Cool for throwing at trees, but NOT at your brother's feet. (Dad was not happy, even though it was an accident. Sorry about your toe, bro!)

3

Man, we were wild on Halloween. Wild and Weird.

I suppose that's why it's often called "Devil's Night."

Those days are gone, but I still love Halloween. Now I usually just get my kids dressed up, take them around the neighborhood for a while, then come back home to hand out candy. Safe, boring, and wonderful.

So with that…Happy Halloween!

Enjoy the issue.

The Storyteller Guy

Ninja—Cesar Valtierra

GO HOME TO READ

Denny Marshall

After **trick-or-treating** on Halloween

Go home to read a scary magazine

Want to go to a friend's house on Fifth & Green

After trick-or-treating on **Halloween**

Sometimes want to be older than preteen

Wish you had your very own **time machine**

After trick-or-treating on Halloween

Go home to read a scary **magazine**

BLACK
CAT

The lamplit moon
falls on his
whiskers

he conducts
his business with
the shadows

then walks
sideways
into the night.

By Giulietta M. Spudich

Art work by Linda and Niem

6

THE HOWLER

Irene Mathias

Last night I lay tucked up in bed, covers to my chin.

You all know what I'm saying – don't let the bedbugs in.

My eyes were closed, my body limp, my name was on a dream.

I had reached the Land of Half-asleep when I heard the Howler

scream!

The terrifying sound leaked in as something screeched my name.

Surely not. A nightmare? AHHHH – there it was again!

Wide awake and scared to move, the Howler smelled my fear.

It shrieked my name out once again and chuckled in my ear.

"*Not real*" I kept repeating and I covered up my head,

While I tried to hatch escape plans. Destination? Parents' bed.

But then it scratched the window as it tried to get inside.

By then I had no choice, I had to find a place to hide.

I'd hardly moved a muscle when the Howler wailed again,

And he battered on the window with the force of twenty men.

I thought the glass was going to break. I dived beneath the bed.

Then suddenly the Howler got right inside my head.

"Pleasssssse let me in" it whispered, *"if you would be so kind.*

I'd like to keep you company – that's if you wouldn't mind?

I promise not to hurt you – well – perhapssss a little bite.

I've filled up on your friend next door, I just need something light."

"A tender little morsel, someone brushed with sssleep will do.

And, my little friend, that snack smells very much like you."

I felt the Howler eyeball me – it gave a squelching wink.

And he scared the wind right out of me (and did it ever stink!)

Statue still I lay there and I willed it to be gone.

I was a prisoner in my bedroom – even *I* knew that was wrong.

In that instant I decided I would stand and face The Fear.

"Bring it on" it heard me whisper and its smile turned to a sneer.

8

I charged across the room and threw my window open wide,

And that Howler blew and blasted as it poured itself inside.

It wrapped me in its icy cloak. It drenched me with each breath.

If this went on much longer I would surely freeze to death!

Then the Howler gusted round me and it whispered in my ear.

"You let me in my little friend! I smell you've lost your fear.

I cannot dine on you just now – you won't taste quite so sweet,

So I'll say goodnight and visit with your friends from down the street."

And as it swooped into the night, it boomed and lit the sky.

"We'll meet again my little friend" I heard the Howler cry.

I closed the window, jumped in bed, once more safe and warm.

Proud that I had faced my fear and bravely faced The Storm.

Art work...

By Denny Marshall

© 2013 Denny E. Marshall

Floppy and Friends

©2013 Denny E. Marshall

LONE VISITOR
By Denny Marshall

A one-man spaceship lands in a parking lot. Crowds gather and police arrive. The single occupant emerges. Officials walk up to the alien and ask all types of questions. After listening patiently for ten minutes the alien starts to cry and said, "I don't know. I'm only six years old."

11

NIGHTTIME MAGIC

Melissa Abramovitz

Darkness can be spooky, full of hidden scary things
Gruesome goblins, creepy crawlers, and flapping bat wings

Monsters that hide in closets tend to jump out at night
Things unseen can seem evil when there is no light

But some parts of darkness are not spooky or frightful
The sunset that brings darkness is truly delightful

Darkness helps us fall asleep and get the sleep we need
It tells night animals to wake up and start to feed

Without darkness, we could not see stars up in the sky
We would miss comets and shooting stars whizzing by

Nighttime opens our world to the universe beyond
So find the bright side when darkness taps its magic wand!

Tombstone—Emma Donnelly

ALL HALLOWS EVE

Amanda Evans
Illustrations by A L Hayes

It's All Hallows Eve, the one night when the dead can roam the

earth.

The one night when spirits are free to torment the living,

When evil can roam the land and wreak havoc

It's just one night…one night when anything can happen

"One hour, we challenge you to sit in the graveyard for one hour,"
the boys said.

"One hour to see if the reaper will surface."

"One hour to see if you're tough enough to be part of our group."

What's an hour, thought Johnny?

Ghosts aren't real and there is no such thing as the reaper.

He'd heard the tales…the stories that went around town of the ghost figure that haunts the graveyard.

The stories say that anyone who spends more than 30 minutes in the graveyard on All Hallows Eve becomes his prey, his target, and they never return.

"I'll do it," said Johnny. "I ain't no chicken."

The boys laughed…"We'll see."

Torch filled with new batteries, phone fully charged

Johnny pushed open the creaky gate to the graveyard.

There was no moon tonight, just complete darkness

The boys moaned and groaned…setting the scene, they said.

But Johnny knew they were trying to scare him.

"One hour," they said, "we'll be back in one hour."

"You ready, Johnny?"

"I'll see you back here in an hour," he said moving forward

What's an hour...it's only 60 minutes

He moved slowly through the **darkness**

Torch on and phone fully charged

What's the worst that can happen?

Settling by an old tombstone he began his wait

An hour…it's only 60 minutes

The silence was eerie, nothing moving, all was deathly still

The darkness everywhere

Only 55 minutes to go

New batteries in his torch and his phone fully charged

Soft moans began to fill the air

His body jumped to attention

"It's just the boys."

50 minutes to go

A sharp scream pierced the air, a woman

He shone his torch in her direction

Nothing there

Only 45 minutes to go

A fog began to descend on the graveyard, thick and gloomy

Rustling of leaves

He shone his torch

Nothing there

Only 40 minutes to go

A loud moan...a bang

Fog surrounding him

Shining the torch

Nothing there

Only 35 minutes to go

The darkness silent once more

The fog still falling

But his torch had new batteries and his phone fully charged

Only 30 minutes to go

A loud bang, more screams and moans

Pointing his torch...nothing...no light

Grabbing his phone...nothing...battery dead

Darkness, screaming

25 minutes to go

Heart racing…"it's just the boys"…"it's just the boys"

Leaves rustling behind him

Heart racing...pulse thumping

It's just the boys…it's just the boys

20 minutes to go

Shadows begin moving

Leaves rustling...even closer now

Complete darkness

Panic ensues

Still 20 minutes to go

Johnny moves

Slowly making his way towards the gate

Darkness all around

No torch…no phone

A thick fog surrounding him

Moans and screams getting louder and louder

"It's just the boys…it's just the boys"

15 minutes to go

A dark shadow coming towards him

Johnny makes to run

Screams and moans fill his ears

His heart racing…his eyes darting around the darkness

"It's just the boys…it's just the boys…"

10 minutes to go

Trying to run through the darkness

Trying to find the gates

Leaves rustling, screams and moans

The dark shadow getting closer

A hand grabs his ankle and drags him to the ground

Panic rising

Hair standing on the back of his neck

A cold chill fills the air

The dark shadow getting closer and closer

5 minutes to go

Panic freezes his body

His hands digging in the dirt

Kicking to release the hold on his ankle

The dark shadow almost on top of him

"It's one of the boys…it's one of the boys"

A scythe cuts through the air

Frozen in terror he watches

A piece of tombstone lands beside him,

The scythe cuts through the air again

"It's one of the boys…it's one of the boys"

Just 2 minutes to go

A loud scream

A chilling laugh

"You're next Johnny…you're next"

"30 minutes is all you get…you're mine now...you're mine"

The scythe getting closer and closer

Head huddled in his hands

Screams fill the air

Laughter…mocking…and the smell of rotting flesh

22

The scythe catches his leg as he crawls towards the gates

I minute to go...I minute to go

"You can't run Johnny…you're mine."

A dark hand reaching for him

The gates in sight

The hand getting closer

Just a little further to go

The gates in sight

The shadow reaching,

The scythe swinging in the air,

And the hand now almost there

The gates…the gates

Reaching out…touching the cold, hard metal

"You can't leave Johnny…30 minutes and you're mine…

you're mine!"

One hand on the gate pulling it open

Reaching out…the glow of the streetlights

Turning…looking into the eyes of death

His heart racing…mind overcome with **fear**

He pulls his frozen body through the gate

A hand grips his leg, pulling him back

"Your mine Johnny…you're mine!"

"There's no escape now…30 minutes is all you get."

The **cold** hand of death

The scythe falling through the air

Piercing his heart

As the last scream leaves his body . . .

"Are you ready, Johnny?"

"60 minutes to prove you're not chicken."

"We'll meet you here when it's over."

Johnny looked…phone fully charged…new batteries in his torch

It's All Hallows Eve, the night of the walking dead

Are you brave enough to spend an hour in the reaper's

graveyard?

©2015 Denny E. Marshall

Head Lock—Denny Marshall

WHEN ALIEN PIGS FLY

By Rebecca Linam

By the shore of the stream that lay right below the central command building, two young Alpha Centauri children were throwing chunks of bread into the water for the lower life forms that called the stream their home. The commander watched them from the window with a smile. The youngest child was his granddaughter.

At the sound of the door opening, he turned. "Ah, Ken Amari! Your report, please? Were the Earthlings grateful for our offer of aid?" The commander folded his four arms across his chest and focused all four of his eyes on Ken Amari. Two of his eyes were detecting nervousness.

Ken Amari cleared his throat, closing two of his eyes. "Our mission to bring aid to the intelligent life called human on the planet Earth was

27

a failure. As Alpha Centaurians, we pride ourselves on giving aid to those in need, but in this instance, I fear it's not possible."

"Not possible?" the commander repeated, glancing back at the window. His granddaughter had just hurled a chunk of bread bigger than her fist at the stream, causing a school of guski to scatter.

Ken Amari clasped two of his hands behind his back. "Well, sir..."

"How could a simple aid mission be a failure?" the commander repeated. "Our reconnaissance teams have determined that a portion of the Earth's population goes hungry, as they do not have enough food supply." His light blue skin had turned a shade darker. "Did you not give them food?"

Ken Amari felt his own blue skin growing paler. "Yes, sir, but..."

"What did you feed them?" the commander demanded, waving two of his arms around in a frenzy.

"We took seven hundred of our antekis with us," Ken Amari mumbled, wringing all four hands together. "They are very similar to the lower life form on Earth called a pig, which many Earthlings breed for food. The only difference is that our antekis have very small wings on their backs. They're no use for flying, although our scientists think that they have evolved to the point that—"

"Stop fidgeting." The commander slapped at Ken Amari's hands. "And stop giving me a science lecture about the anteki. Were the antekis not agreeable to the Earthlings' stomachs?"

Ken Amari sighed. "I don't know. They never ate them."

The commander turned back to the window, mumbling something about blowing 25% of the Alpha Centauri budget. "Stupid aid team. Even a small Alpha Centaurian knows how to throw crumbs to the creatures in the lakes and streams! Should I have sent my five-year-old granddaughter with you to demonstrate?" he added, pointing out the window.

The two children were chunking pieces of bread the size of rocks into the stream. They had mastered the art of giving aid.

By now, Ken Amari's blue skin was almost as pale as that of some Earthlings. "Actually, we did just that. We stopped in a field above a group of Earthlings. They were kicking a checkered ball around—don't really know the significance of that custom yet. Anyway, we had our cloaking device turned on to match the clouds, and at the signal, we threw the antekis down like bread crumbs to the Earthlings."

The commander looked puzzled. "And they did not accept them?"

Ken Amari shook his head. "All seven hundred antekis fell to the ground with their tiny wings breaking gravity, but the minute they hit the field, the Earthlings scattered. A few antekis even landed right on top of the Earthlings, but did they thank us? No. They just lay there on the ground without moving."

"They ran?" The commander scratched his head with three of his arms. "And played dead?"

Ken Amari nodded. "I don't think they're ready for contact with us."

The commander's skin had returned back to its normal shade of blue. "Maybe not," he said with a sigh. "They don't even know how to appreciate our gesture of kindness. Thank you, Ken Amari. I'll try to think of a better tactic."

He turned back to the window with all four hands clasped behind his back; sometimes it wasn't easy being the most intelligent species in the universe.

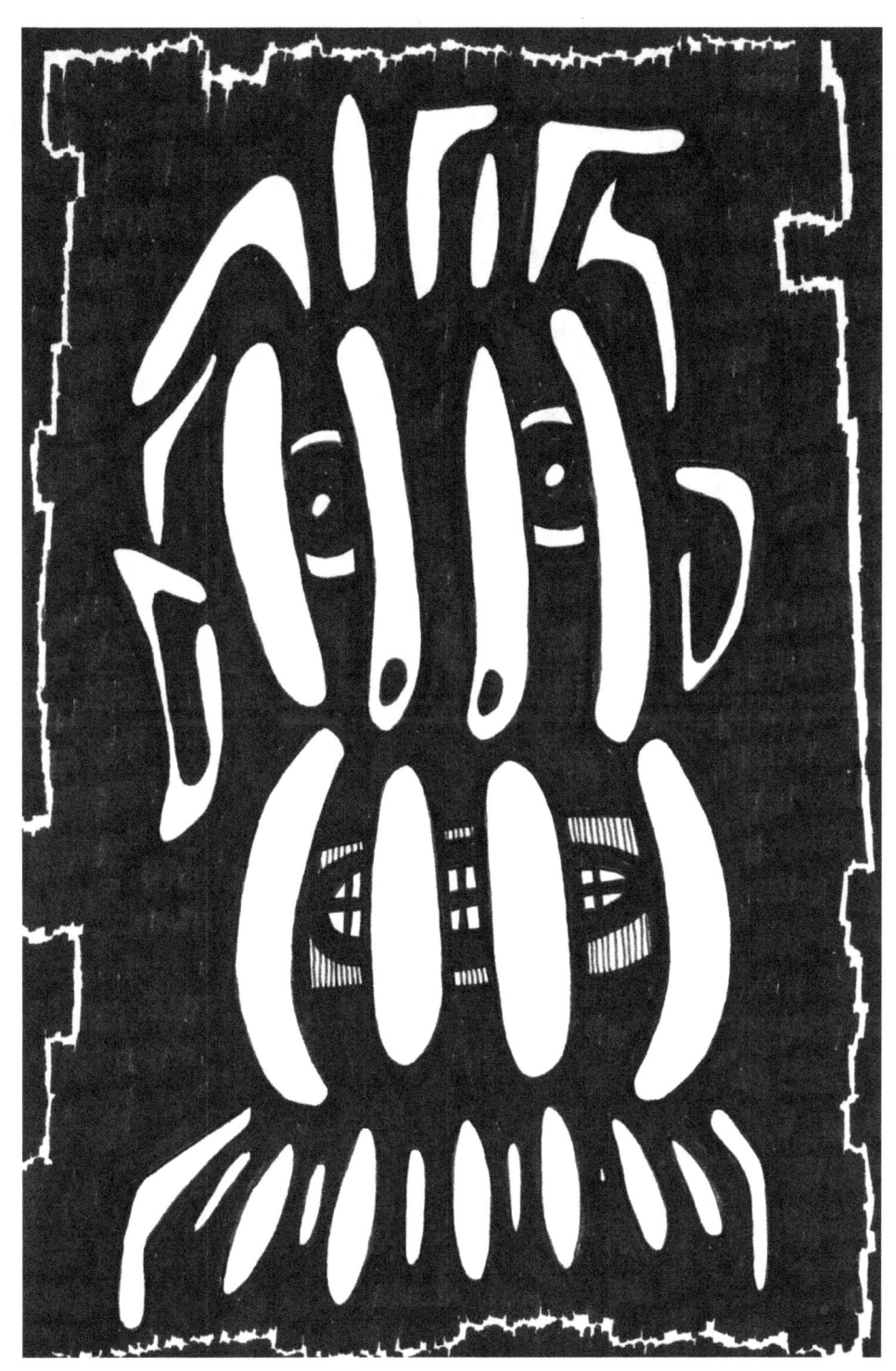

Break the Wall—Denny Marshall

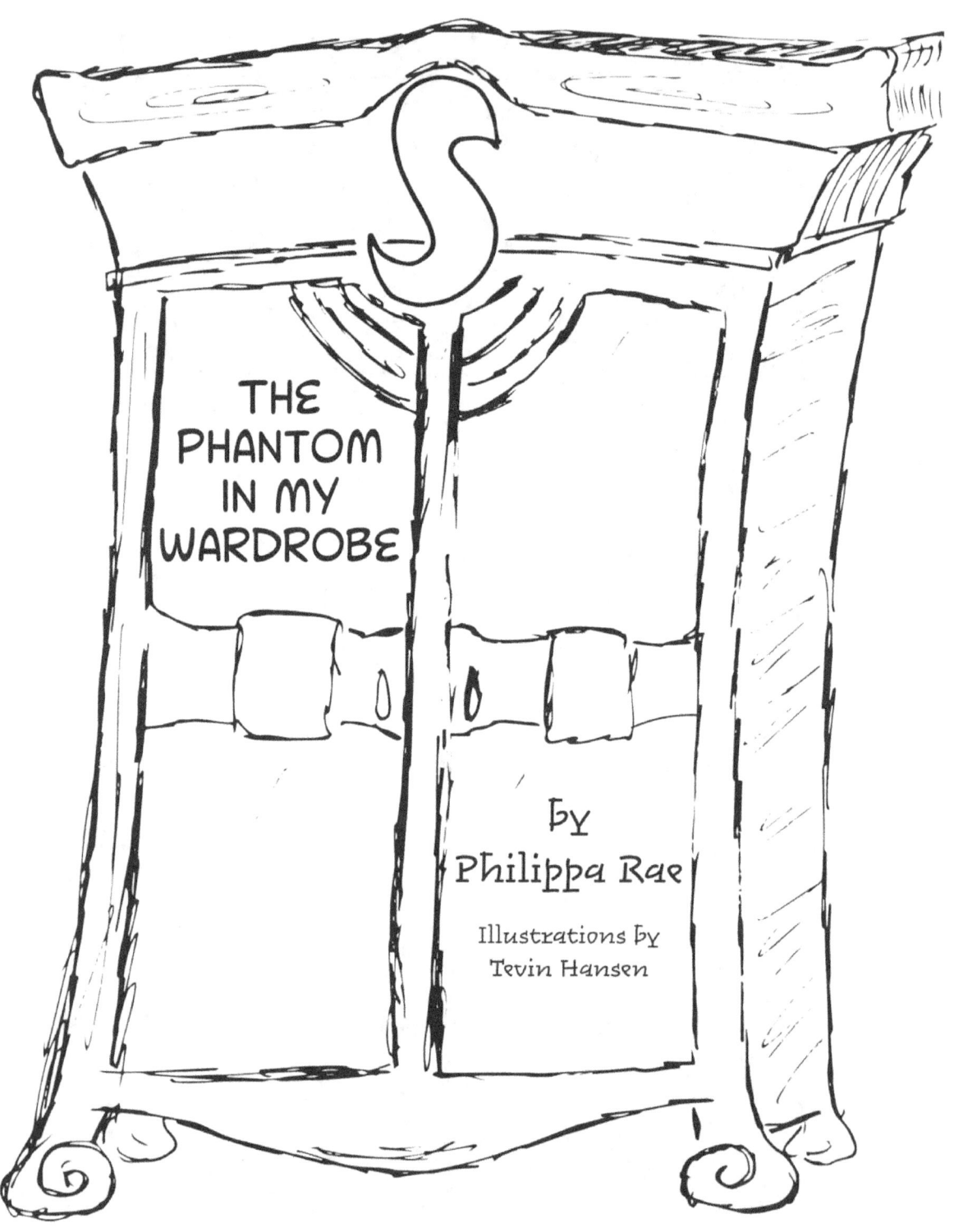

THE
PHANTOM
IN MY
WARDROBE

by

Philippa Rae

Illustrations by
Tevin Hansen

There's a phantom in my wardrobe
An unrested pest lives there
At night transforms my bedroom
As she hunts for clothes to wear

My carpet is her catwalk
As she duets with my attire
My garments are possessed
What else does she require?

The wardrobe doors burst open
Then loudly they slam shut
Whoosh! Once again they open
Out march clothes with a strut

She gives my belts a rattle

Discorded melody of zips

Buttons pop, Velcro rasps

As the spectra strips

This errant soul spooks my gloves

Slither, creep and crawl

Hats hover headlessly

As they rise and fall

Across the ceiling my slacks run

As if chased by a curse

But a pair of jeans is quicker

Boo! They reach the lampshade first

My leotard gets active

When did ghosts start keeping fit?

I thought they hated exorcise

Now my tracksuit's split!

It's a **scary**, hairy vision

Clothes levitate in a line
Beat of heart is missed
There's a tingle in my spine

Soon I had my fill
Of this nightmare fright
I overcame my terror
At this freaky sight

I summoned up the courage.
"Can I help?" Nervously I said
She replied "I thought you'd never ask
Have you any size twelves instead?"

SPACE FAIRY FABLE:

Winston Van Lance

Billy, the Cyborg Leprechaun,
Plays a magical fiddle.

Purchased from an Evil Witch,
Her payment was a riddle.

The rhyme spoke of an ancient clan of Vampires from Mars.
Claimed to be quite powerful,
With an Empire throughout the stars.

Billy, the Cyborg Leprechaun,
Has a flying galleon made of gold.

With a band of Fair Folk Minstrels,
Most adventurous and bold.

They travel towards forbidden lands,
In search of ancient spells.
A quest foretold most dangerous...
Legends proclaim it'll end in hell!

Kart—Cesar Valtierra

SMALL STEPS

Andrea Cox Christen

The two little girls lived with their mom and their dad far away from their house, but were still at home. Though they had traveled a long way, it didn't feel too long because Ren had Butterfly Baby and Marlet had Baby Luke. As long as there was Butterfly Baby with her plastic smile and her polyester wings, and Baby Luke's bald head and faded pajamas—and Mama and Dada of course—then nothing was too far away. Even though the stars looked completely different, and the number of moons had changed, each night Marlet and Ren fell asleep in their government-issued homestead hearing the familiar noises: Dada's snoring, Mama's shifting in her bed, Marlet sucking on her thumb, Ren muttering in her sleep. Big things were different, but the little things, the things that made anywhere home, were still the same.

That was true, at least, until one night when Marlet woke up and felt a pressure in her tummy. She had to pee, so she climbed up from her pad, and went through the portal. Holding her hands in front of her, she felt her way to the weclamation pod, using the light from the glowing plants to get down the hall. Marlet was a big girl now. She

38

could find the weclamation pod and even sometimes find the right sensors on the machine in the dark. She was still too short for some of them, but she tried. Sometimes in the morning Mama would say, "Who didn't release their pee?" But those times didn't happen too much now. She was getting big.

As she walked back to her portal, she tried to inch her pajama legs down over her heels so her feet didn't get cold on the hard metal floor. The green glow from the plantarium lit her way back to her room, but then she heard a sound.

"Schhuff, schuuf." It echoed down off the metal walls.

What could that be? thought Marlet.

"Schuuff, schhhuuu." It came again.

Marlet's stomach tightened. She leaned into the dark, trying to see more in the little light the plants emitted. All that she could see looked right. The hallway seemed empty. The portal to her room was open like it would be until she re-entered. The plants in the plantarium raised their leaves in silence.

But the sound was not right. It sounded like something stuck in the weclamation pod pipes, but it wasn't coming from there. Could it be something in the bentilation shaft? Mama and Dada had said something about that after the last big rain. Marlet wasn't sure what a bentilation shaft was, but maybe it made that slippy, airy sound.

"Schuff," the sound came again, but this time there was a great pause. Then, "Schuufff."

Marlet's fingers twisted in her pants, and she jigged from leg to leg. It felt like she had to pee, but she'd just gone in the weclamation pod. Why weren't there more glowing plants so she could see better at night? Why were the light sensors made for tall people? Why was it so hard to be small?

Oh! She could call Dada! He'd take care of the thing in the bentilation shaft. He knew what to do with the purple insects that crawled out of the faucet and the hairy, bread-loaf shaped animal that had been sitting on their table when they came back to their homestead after a weekend trip. He could help!

But if she called for Dada, the thing would know where she was. It might jump on her and bite her. It might steal her away from her family. It might lick her face with its acid tongue. Right now, in the dark she was safe. Alone and scared, but she wasn't found. The thing in the shaft didn't know she was standing right outside of the weclamation pod, and she was a good hider, just ask her sister.

Ren had taught her to be good at hide-and-seek. Even on small transport ships they could play, and because they could both tuck into places and be so quiet they were so good at this game. Marlet could be the quietest, and she wasn't going to let any green monster hiding in the bentilation shaft scare her.

"Schuffk! Schuuu," the noise got louder. Marlet took a tiny breath and stood very still. Maybe it could sense movement. Ren had told her about the Broltollian monkey that could sense movement though it had no real eyes. Maybe a Broltollian monkey had gotten into the bentilation shaft. Those monkeys had scary faces. They had no eyes, just a blank spot where their peepers should be and that spot was covered in fur. To see one in the dark would be too scary.

Oh, her feet were getting so cold. Marlet wanted to rub them on each other, but then she'd be moving. The Broltollian monkey would sense the movement and then it'd be trying to hug her like the one Ren said tried to squeeze kids at recess at her new school. It might press its hairy face right next to her eyes and then she'd scream so loud even Mama would wake up. Oh, why didn't the stupid monkey go away?

The pattern on the metal floor felt like rocks stabbing into her. How long had she been standing in the hall, looking into the green glow?

41

Why couldn't she just move and see if the sound stopped?

"Be brave like Dada," she thought to herself. She tried to think of her Dada, but all she could see in her mind was a Broltollian monkey face, hairy and round with only a mouth and small slits for a nose.

"I'm big! I'm big! So big!" she told herself silently.

She inched her foot forward. Then the other.

"Schuuff. Skhuff." The sound didn't really change as she crept toward her room. Marlet let out her breath and loosened her shoulders.

Marlet knew what she'd do as soon as she got to the door. She'd rush through it, waving at the "Close" button and then dive onto her pad. Nothing could get her then. How many steps to go? Five? Twelve? Numbers were so confusing in the dark.

Oh, no! Marlet's ear clung to the air. Yes, it was true! The noise was getting louder.

"Schukkk! Skuuf!"

The noise seemed to be coming from her own room. Had the monkey climbed out of the bentilation shaft? Was it sitting in her bed? If it thought it was going to hurt her sister, it was wrong. No one hurt Ren if Marlet could stop it.

What if it was sleeping on her pad? It was going to need a new place to sleep because it was Marlet's and Baby Luke's pad, and no one else's. Not even Mama was allowed on Marlet's pad.

What if it was playing with Baby Luke? No one could do that. Not even Ren.

Marlet vaulted into the room, jumping up and down in front of the "Illuminate" button. The light panels slid down, flooding the room with watts. Marlet's eyes stung in the sudden light, but she tried to see what invader was on her pad, hurting her sister or her doll. Baby Luke was under the blanket. Everything was normal.

"Hey, what are you doin', Mar? It's time to sleep still," Ren said, coughing a bit.

"There was a Broltollian monkey on my pad! It was playing with Baby Luke!"

Ren rolled over and looked at her sister's pad. "Your doll looks like she's sleeping to me. Are you sure you didn't dream it?" Ren rubbed her eyes in the glaring light.

"No, I heard it coming back from the weclamation pod," Marlet said. Her eyebrows dashed her face in concentration.

"Okay," said Ren. "Let's just check, okay?"

Ren turned to the panel near her head and gestured, swiping

through records. "Is this what you heard?" She made a quick tapping motion at the panel.

"Schukkk! Skuuf!"

"Yeah, that's it! See. I told you so!"

"Sounds kinda like Dada. Let's see about that." Ren turned to the panel and said, "Identify sound."

"Sound identified: Snoring," said the computer panel.

"So you just heard Dada, Marlet. See?"

"But Dada's not here." Marlet crossed her arms.

Ren frowned. "Identify snorer," she told the panel.

"Ren Larken."

Marlet laughed, and waved the lights down. "You snore like Dada, Ren!" She cuddled under the blanket, smiling to herself. Her big sister made as much noise as Dada. She sounded like a big daddy instead of a small girl.

"Ren snores. Ren snores!" she thought to herself as she cuddled in her blanket, pulling Baby Luke close.

And then she wondered why her bald baby doll had so much hair.

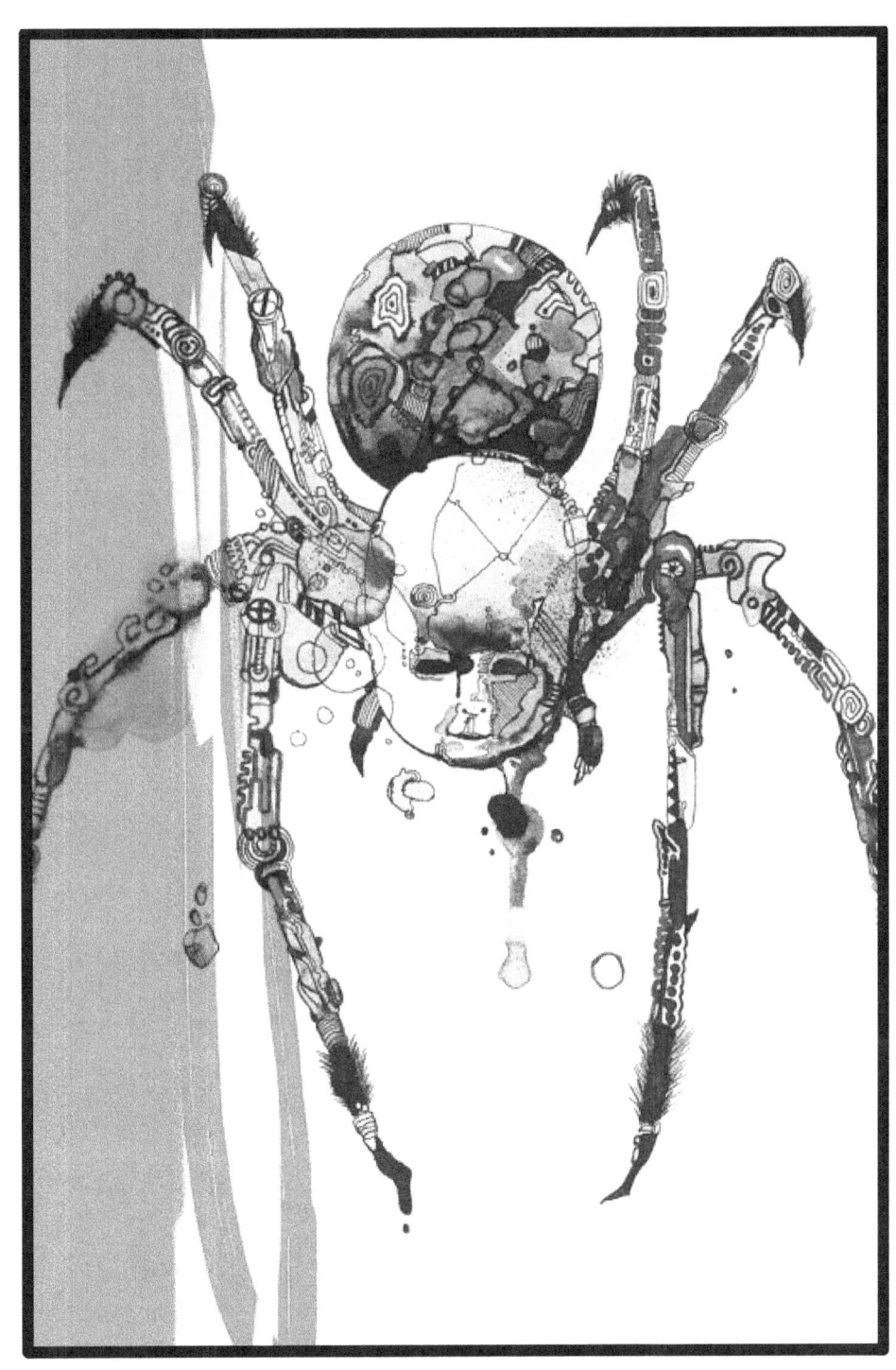

Spider Baby—Cesar Valtierra

Shadow—Emma Donnelly

SHADOW MASTER

Irene Mathias

There's something in the corner, by the window, near the door.
Its tongue is sticking out; black fangs drip something on the floor!

Its head ends in a point, broad shoulders hunch as arms spread wide.
Its stomach moves in waves as if there's someone caught inside!

As one eye winks sharp claws reach out, it leans towards my bed!
I scream before the Shadow Master bites off half my head!

I hear my dad run from his room and thunder down the hall.
My light goes on and suddenly…there's nothing there at all!

He said my clothes piled on the chair cast shapes upon the wall.
"You're really seeing something that just isn't there at all."

He tucks me in and lifts the clothes then dumps them on the floor.
He switches off my light, "Goodnight," and shuts my bedroom door.

There's something in the corner, by the window, near the door.
It tried to eat me once tonight and now it's back for more!

UNTITLED

fast food advances
chicken nuggets are hatched
already deep-fried

UNTITLED

she clones brain tissue
a brilliant gift to satisfy
her zombie lover

UNTITLED

vernal equinox
day becomes longer than night
undead hibernate

OUT OF HADES

Persephone's cat
counts the days to equinox
coolness of summer.

Poems by:
Herb Kauderer

Triangle Guy—Denny Marshall

THE SHORT STRAW
Irene Mathias

Flashlight—Emma Donnelly

Halloween, my favourite day.
Home from school, no time to play.

Costume on, fangs in place.
Long black cloak, pale white face.

Doorbell rings. Friends are here!
Ghost and Mummy show no fear.

Cloudy sky. Wispy fog.
Orange moon. Howling dog.

Trick or Treat, door to door.
Bags are full, stomach sore!

Main event, end of town.
Everybody gathers round.

Haunted House - Blackbrick Lane.
Heard the owners went insane!

Draw straws. Short one's mine!
Check my watch, is that the time?

"Bedroom window on the right,
Stand and wave, flash this light."

Iron gates, opened wide.
Close my eyes. Step inside!

Gather courage. Stalk the path.
Crowd let out a nervous laugh.

Climb the steps. One, two, three.
Chicken out? No! Not me!

Door opens! Autumn breeze?
Blood inside me starts to freeze.

Feet won't move - stuck to mat.
Someone shouts *"scaredy cat."*

Cotton mouth. Filled with dread.
Stumble forward, legs like lead.

House **dark**, awful smell.
Might be me - hard to tell!

Flashlight on, look around.
Dusty footprints on the ground!

Staircase looms, long and black.
Start to climb, can't go back.

Creak and groan from every stair.
Spiders fill the cobwebbed air.

Reach the top - Look around.
Lots of doors - Not a sound.

Tiptoe slowly down the hall.
Something scuttles up the wall!

Noise behind me, spin around!
Fresh footprints on the ground!

Bigger steps - Reach the room.
Heart beats wildly - Boom, boom, boom.

Reach the window! Flash and wave
Crowd applaud. Feeling brave!

Door bangs! Curtains blow!
Petrified! Time to go!

Cupboard opens with a creak.
Try to scream - can only squeak!

Something whispers from within,
"Welcome home. Come on in."

Silent air breathes a moan.
Now I'm in the terror zone!

Launch my body through the door.
Feet don't hardly touch the floor!

Stumble blindly down the hall.
Pictures staring from the wall!

Moving shadows cloak the stair.
Definitely something there!

Attack the stairs, two by two.
Something grabs my running shoe!

Drop my torch, lunge for the door.
Crowd all cheer. *"RUN!"* I roar.

Rocket home, super-fast!
Tucked in bed. Safe at last.

Noise outside. Night's alive!
Imagination overdrive?

Next day, feeling better.
Heading out. Grab a sweater.

Open door, and on the porch,
Sit running shoe and broken torch!

CUENTOS DE NOCHE
(NIGHT TALES)
By Janitzi Alvarez

Old Mexican legends and myths

Are what my mother would tuck me into bed with

Oh, all the stories she would tell

Some of which scared me all too well

She'd say if I stayed up too late at night,

'El Cucuy', a boogeyman, would sweep into sight

Or the story of the ghost woman who would weep

Because her children drowned in the river deep

Then there was the myth that those random bruises found

Are caused by witches sucking on your soul from all around

Or the tales of trickster elves

That would scurry up and down your bed and shelves

Of course as I grew older,

My logic warmed up and imagination got colder

My days of believing those stories were gone and dead

Until one night I awoke to a witch floating over my bed

Cemetery Gates—Emma Donnelly

55

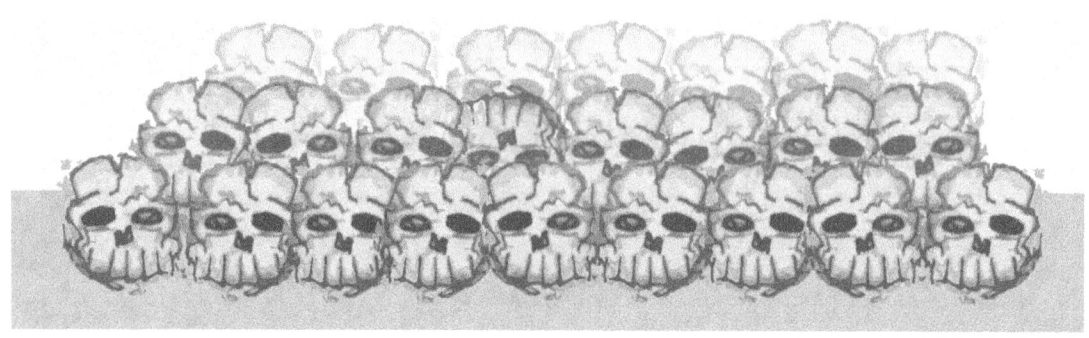

AUTHORS, POETS, AND ILLUSTRATORS

Melissa Abramovitz is an award-winning author who specializes in writing nonfiction books and magazine articles for all age groups, from preschoolers through adults. She also dabbles in poetry, fiction, and picture books and has numerous publications in these areas as well.

Janitzi Alvarez is a 12th grade student at Stonewall Jackson High School. Her writing reflects her Mexican-American culture, which she appreciates very much. With sports, school, and work, writing is still a hobby she tries to keep up with.

Andrea Cox Christen's father was a photogrammetrist (a person who makes maps from aerial photography), so maps were a part of her childhood. As an adult, she decided to explore beyond the map of her Montana hometown, so she and her family packed nine suitcases and moved to Indonesia where she teaches, reads, and writes.

Emma Donnelly is a thirteen-year-old artist from Ireland. Emma was one of the winners of the 2016 My Ireland Poetry competition and had her winning entry published along with the artwork to accompany it. Emma's goal is to be an animation specialist and illustrator.

AUTHORS, POETS, AND ILLUSTRATORS CONTINUED

Amanda J Evans is a freelance writer, poet, and author. Amanda lives in Oldcastle, Co. Meath, Ireland with her husband and two children. She is known locally by her married name Donnelly but she writes under her maiden name Evans. She has been published in Wildflower Muse, Mused: Bella Online Literary Review Magazine, Visual Verse, and a number of other journals. She is also the author of Surviving Suicide: A Memoir from Those Death Left Behind, published in 2012. When she is not writing content for her business clients, she's most likely reading the latest novels to hit the newsstands and sharing snippets from her latest manuscripts with her husband and their two children. Amanda also teaches a children's writing group in the small village where she lives and is an active member of an adult writing group also. You can find out more on her website www.amandajevans.com

A L Hayes was born and raised in Dublin, Ireland, but now lives a quieter life in the beautiful countryside of Co Meath. Following a bad car accident in 2014, she decided to return to her teenage pursuits of writing and painting, and has only begun to put her work into the public domain. Most of her paintings are carried out in acrylic on canvas. One of her greatest passions in life is animal welfare and she has donated prizes of Pet Portraits to be auctioned to raise funds to care for abandoned pets.

Herb Kauderer has four children, but would read kids' books even if he didn't have kids. He is an associate professor of English at Hilbert College where he sometimes gets to teach cool courses such as Detective Fiction, and The Literature of Horror

AUTHORS, POETS, AND ILLUSTRATORS CONTINUED

Winston Van Lance is a nerdy guy in his early twenties from California. He loves tea, hates ketchup, and seems to always name his pets after reggae artists.

Rebecca Linam teaches German at the University of North Alabama. Her stories have appeared in "Skipping Stones," "Spaceports and Spidersilk," "Lights and Shadows," and "Funny in Five Hundred." For more information, visit her website at www.rebeccalinam.com or find her on Twitter @rebecca_linam.

Linda and **Niem** like to draw together with cats being a favorite subject.

Denny Marshall has had art, poetry, and fiction published. One recent credit would be cover art for *Disturbed Digest* June 2015; the other half of the drawing is on the back cover. See more at www.dennymarshall.com

Irene Mathias currently resides in Paisley, Scotland with her husband and daughter (whom she takes great pleasure in scaring with her "after dark" tales). By day Irene is a Project Manager who devotes what little time she has left to writing all manner of children's poetry. She has had success in local, national and international competitions and is currently compiling her first collection of fright-time stories, "Scared? Me?" of which The Short Straw, Shadow Master and The Howler form part.

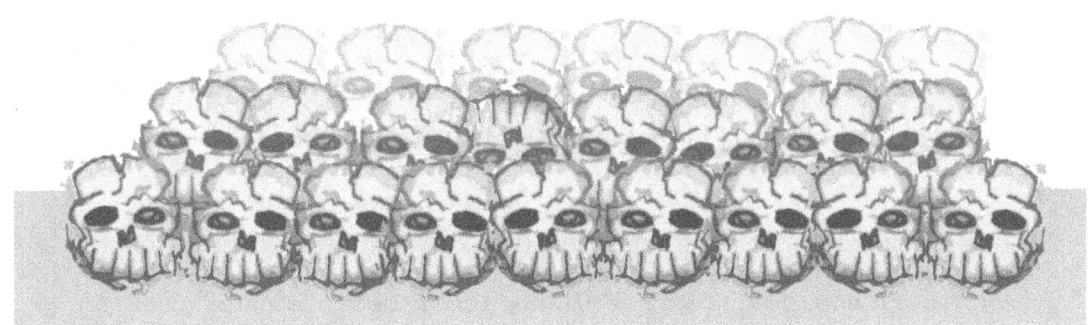

AUTHORS, POETS, AND ILLUSTRATORS CONTINUED

Philippa Rae has had many short stories and poems broadcast on BBC Children's radio, and she has also written for television. As well as contributing to a number of anthologies and magazines she has had success in many local and national competitions such as the Moondance International Festival. Her picture book Count the Sheep to Sleep won a silver award at the Moonbeam Children's Book Awards.

Giulietta M Spudich: I love to write, and I love the sea. I run all my poems by my friendly cat Smokey, who either nods in approval or twitches his tail.

Cesar Valtierra, mail@cesarvaltierra.com of El Paso, TX, is a graphic artist who really enjoys creating all types of great art and working on his comic, Balazo, which can be found at www.tonybalazo.com. He is currently looking to flesh out his portfolio by doing illustrative work and welcomes anyone in need of that (www.orderfromkhaos.com and www.cesarvaltierra.com). He lives with his fiancée Victoria, who is the love of his life and his inspiration and muse, and their two cats: Chubs and Pretty Boy.

THANK YOU'S

As always, we want to thank our very talented contributors for another great issue. Without them there would be no Stinkwaves. If you would like to be a part of our accomplished crew, visit www.stinkwavesmagazine.com for submission guidelines, or email us at submissions@stinkwavesmagazine.com with any questions.

Follow us on Facebook and Twitter to stay up to date on the latest Stinkwaves shenanigans.

Handersen Publishing, LLC is an independent publishing house.

We hope you enjoyed this issue and will consider supporting our many talented contributors by leaving a review on Amazon, or even purchasing some of our back issues on Kindle.

Thank you.

Handersen Publishing, LLC
Lincoln, Nebraska

MORE YOUNG ADULT, MIDDLE GRADE, AND PICTURE BOOKS FROM OUR TALENTED CONTRIBUTORS:

ABCs of Health and Safety by Melissa Abramovitz, Guardian Angel Publishing. This is a picture book that uses alphabet-linked words and delightful rhymes to introduce children to important health and safety tips. From active aerobics to heart healthy habits to zoo zone zeal, kids will have fun while learning on this A-Z journey. Fun illustrations by Alexander Morris enhance the text in this picture book; recommended for ages 4-8. www.melissaabramovitz.com

The Best Mariachi in the World by J.D. Smith and Dani Jones Delta Publishing Company: Raven Tree Press (Picture Book)

Everyone in Gustavo's family is in a mariachi band. Everyone except Gustavo, that is. They all play violínes, trompetas and guitarrones. Gustavo would love to join the band, but he can't play any of the instruments. This book is available in English or Spanish, and also embedded (English with Spanish sprinkled throughout) editions.

Black Fox In Thin Places by Scáth Beorh Emby Press (Middle Grade)

The Tolkien-esque adventures of Sionnach Varela, a 17th Century Irish girl who seemingly stumbles upon a noble denizen of that country's most famous folk, the Sidhe.

Count the Sheep to Sleep by Philippa Rae, Sky Pony Press (Picture Book)

In this amusing bedtime story, a little girl decides she must count sheep in order to fall asleep. Starting at ten, her sheep begin to suffer humorous mishaps as she happily drifts into dreamland. Each number illustrates sheep flying off in different directions, unable to control their skateboards, the slippery floor, or their crazy dance moves. Children will laugh and learn in this combination bedtime and counting book.

Fireheart by Giulietta Spudich, Books to Go Now (YA)

Eighteen-year old Ariana is frustrated by her inability to contribute to her forest band as she is chained to a large, though friendly, dragon. Now she must keep the dragon and the Light People safe from the human race.

The First Americans by Kelly Bakshi, Guardian Angel Publishing, Inc. (Middle Grade)

Would you use a buffalo bladder as a canteen or wear a coat made out of seal skin? Native Americans cleverly used everything in their environment in order to survive.

Grimly Jane by Elle Alexander, Oliver Press LLC (Middle Grade)

Jane Worthington is an orphan who has been cruelly treated by everyone. When one day she is locked away as usual, she discovers a secret door to another world. Crawling through it, she begins a mysterious and exciting journey that will change her life forever.

Helping Herbie Hedgehog by Melissa Abramovitz, Guardian Angel Publishing, Inc. (Picture Book)

Herbie the clueless hedgehog needs help figuring out how to get places and go about his day. Amusing delightful rhymes invite kids to give helpful advice while learning about everyday things. www.melissaabramovitz.com

The Journey of the Nightisans by Rebecca Linam, iUniverse (YA)

Lucasse Koltz, the world's most arrogant guy, ends up cursing the world in an attempt to impress the ladies. He and his ragtag team of friends must save the day—including a magician who is allergic to magic, a mad scientist in training, and a talking cat. But someone out there wants to stop Lucasse from breaking the curse, and that person turns out to be a shadow from his past. Young Adult, 264 pages.

Myth-Busting Columbus by Kelly Bakshi Guardian Angel Publishing, Inc. (Middle Grade)

Columbus convinced royals to fund his voyage. He forged new water routes and introduced Europe to a new world. He also lied to his crew, murdered and enslaved Native Americans, and never realized where in the world he actually was. You decide, is he a hero or a villain?

Nine Digits by Jay Duret, Second Wind Publishing (Middle Grade)

Nee-Nee Marcus is a headstrong, self-absorbed, 15-year-old who despises her family. She would do anything to be free of them. When she hears about a new reality television program that will award a prize of $100 million, she decides she'll do whatever it takes to win. www.ninedigits.com.

Olives—*20th Anniversary Edition* by Herb Kauderer (Poetry)

Just in time for Halloween, a collection of dark poetry. Available on Kobo.com

She Dreamed of Dragons by Elizabeth J. M. Walker, Mirror World Publishing (YA).

Trina is a dragon mage in a kingdom ruled by witches and wizards. In an effort to find a suitable teacher to help control her fire powers, she enters The Royal Tourney—a competition to find the next successor to the throne.

Shonim by Giulietta Spudich (YA)

Sarah is bored at her family's summer home in the countryside, until she discovers a fairy in her garden. Despite her family's disbelief and the fairy tribe's fear, they become fast friends. Books I-V free on Bibliotastic.

The Truth About Snails by JD DeHart (Poetry)

Ordinary objects take on a new form, and myths become real and move next door in the verses contained in this poem collection. Much of the writing was inspired by comic books and science fiction, and on concepts beyond the scope of the real world, and cast firmly in the supernatural.

The War on State Street by Rebecca Linam, iUniverse (Middle Grade)

Eight-year-old Ester Sandbourne's neighbors, the Thrashers, steal her bicycle, smash her homemade teepee, and make life miserable for everyone on State Street. This means war—a wacky, messy mud ball and rotten tomato fight! Will Ester and her friends be able to defend State Street, or will the Thrashers terrorize State Street for the rest of the summer? Middle Grade; 140 pages with illustrations by Nathan Harper.

Handersen Publishing
Great books for young readers
www.handersenpublishing.com

More books from
Handersen Publishing, LLC

The Evil Mouse Chronicles (Middle Grade)

Mr. B Presents Series (Young Adult)

Middle Grade

Picture Books

www.ingramcontent.com/pod-product-compliance
Lightning Source LLC
Chambersburg PA
CBHW080753120626
46557CB00005B/1256